MIRROR, MIRROR

by Michael Holt
Illustrator: David Brown

Mills and Boon Limited, London

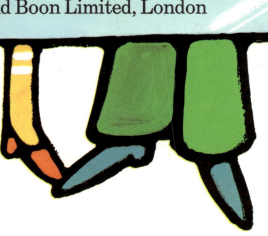

First published in Great Britain 1973 by Mills & Boon Limited,
17-19 Foley Street, London W1A 1DR.

© Michael Holt 1973

© Illustrations Mills & Boon Limited 1973

All rights reserved. No part of this publication may be reproduced, stored
in a retrieval system, or transmitted in any form or by any means,
electronic, mechanical, photocopying, recording or otherwise, without the
prior permission of Mills & Boon.

ISBN 0 263. 05434.9

Made & Printed in Great Britain by Colour Reproductions Ltd,
Billericay, Essex.

What is a mirror?
Of course you've seen
yourself in one.
A mirror shows you
yourself.

But do you know how
a mirror works?
It can do strange things.

See if you can do this puzzle:
Sam can see Sue in the mirror.

Can Sue see Sam in the mirror?
Read this book to find out.
You'll find lots more about mirrors.

What are the best mirrors?
Flat ones or bulgy ones?
Are they made of glass or metal?

Look at a shiny kettle.
Can you see yourself in it?
Look at a spoon . . .
on both sides.
See how your face changes!

Look in a puddle of water.
Can you see yourself?

Look into the bath water.
Is it a mirror?

Look into a friend's eye –
a human's or a dog's.
Can you see yourself?
If so, his eye is a mirror.
Can you see the window too?

Which of these things are mirrors?

a river on a calm day
a goldfish bowl
a television screen (when it's off)
a car fender
a window pane
a shop window
a puddle
a puddle on a windy day

What does the wind do
to the puddle?

A mirror that curves in makes things look smaller.
Sam is looking into the front of the spoon.
Does it make his face look bigger or smaller?

Dad's shaving mirror also curves in.
It makes his face look bigger when he is close to it.
But when he is far away his face looks upside down.

Sue is looking into a flat mirror.

Which picture of herself does she see?

Turn the page and find out.

Sue sees the middle picture in a flat mirror.
Well, which mirrors are best?
Flat ones or bulgy ones?
Are they made of metal or glass?

Where would she see the other pictures?
The top picture: in the back of a spoon, kettle or fender.

The bottom picture: in the front of a spoon, or a shaving mirror.

Here's how to make a flat mirror.
Find a box lid
and some shiny foil.
Cut out a big oblong from the foil.
Tape it smooth and flat to the lid.
You have a mirror.

Look at a friend in your home-made mirror as in our picture.

Can your friend see you in the mirror?

First guess. Then check with your mirror. Now you can solve the puzzle on page 3? Hold your mirror to this page!

.rorrim eht ni maS ees nac euS ,seY

In the story Snow White the Queen said:

"Mirror, mirror, on the wall.
"Who is the fairest one of all?"

Did she see a pretty face or an ugly face?

Hold a mirror to this page:

If you stare you can see both a young girl and an old woman.

The artist has made
two mistakes
in this drawing.

Can you find them?
Hold your mirror here
to see what they are:
Sue's bow and Sam's
– hand in his pocket –
both on wrong side.

What is wrong with this picture?

Go and look in a mirror!

Here's a puzzle.

Can Sam here roll the ball
to Sue?
He can't throw it over the wall.
He mustn't move
and she mustn't move.
There's a gap between fence and wall.

Try it yourself
or work it out.

Which way does he throw it?

1   forward?

2   on a slant?

3   sideways?

What happens then?

Sam rolls the ball on a slant.
Then the ball bounces off the wall
towards Sue.
It comes off the wall at an angle:
the same angle as it hit the wall.

"That must be how light
bounces off a mirror," said Sue.

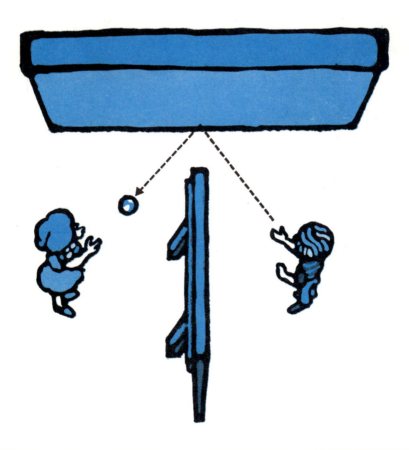

Here's a puzzly puzzle.

Sam shines his torch
at the mirror, like this.

What does Sue see
in the mirror.

She is looking along the dotted line.

She sees the torch.

The torch light bounces off the mirror
and shines in her face.

That's how sunlight bounces
off the Moon at us.
The Moon is a poor mirror.
Moonlight is bounced-off sunlight.

Prop up your mirror on a table.
While looking at your face in it,
walk slowly back as far as you can.
Can you see more of yourself now?

Ask a friend to see if you walked
in a straight line?
Did your mirror "you" walk towards you
or away from you?

A famous artist used mirror-writing
so others could not read what he had written.

Hold a mirror to this page to read his name:

iɔniV ab obɹɒnoǝꓶ

You try to write while looking in a mirror.
It's not easy!

Here's a very puzzly puzzle.

Hold your right ear:
In the mirror, your hand touches
your left ear.

Now face the other way round.

Do as your mirror hand did.

You see, it was the left ear in the mirror.

A mirror swops left with right.

Ever made an ink blot? Good!

Fold a scrap of paper
then open it out flat again.
Drop ink on the fold.
Fold the paper again,
squeeze it hard
and open it once more.

Hold one half up to a mirror.

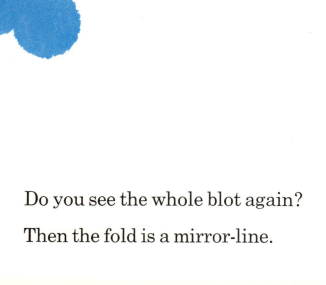

Do you see the whole blot again?

Then the fold is a mirror-line.

Hold a mirror on these shapes
and so find their mirror-lines:
butterfly, star, triangle, square, cherries, jet

Hold a mirror to our dog
and make him longer.

Make him a dog with two tails!

Place several things in a pattern in front of a mirror.

Behind the mirror make the pattern you see in the mirror.

Then take away the mirror.

What do you see?

Try other patterns.

Stand two mirrors in Plasticine
next to each other.

Put a dice near them.

How many dice can you see
in the mirror?

Try it with
two sugar cubes.

Now put some blocks behind the mirrors
where the mirror dice seem to be.
Take the mirrors away.
What pattern do you see?

Close up the mirrors bit by bit.

What happens to the patterns?

Sue can turn herself upside down with two mirrors:

You try it and see.

"Can I turn myself
side to side?" Sue asks.

Can she?

You find out.

Sue has broken her comb.

But Sam mends it for her – with a mirror! How?

He puts his mirror down somewhere and he sees a mended comb.

Where does he put the mirror?

Sam threw mud at the washing!
Can you clean it
with a mirror?

Here it is, spotless.

Sue makes two eggs out of one.

She puts the mirror down somewhere
and she sees two eggs.

But Sam makes three eggs
out of two!

Where does he put the mirror?

Brenda and Timothy went to a party.

They wrote their names on card.

Look at them in a mirror.

What do you see?

Why does that happen?

Turn the page to see.

Answer

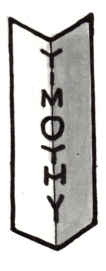

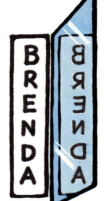

The letters of "Timothy" are the same on each side. When the mirror swops them over, nothing happens. But it does with the name "Brenda".

Find other letters that don't swop over in a mirror.

Find things in the house that do swop over in a mirror.

How can Sue see Sam round the corner?

Here's a secret message
from Sam and Sue.

WE HOPE YOU HAD FUN!

Can you read it
by using a mirror?
– like this

She uses a spy mirror –
like the periscope
submarines use.

Her Dad has a periscope
on his caravan.

With it he can see
what's coming up
behind the caravan.